What's For Breakfast?

Written by Paul Shipton
Illustrated by Jon Stuart

Collins

2

4

5

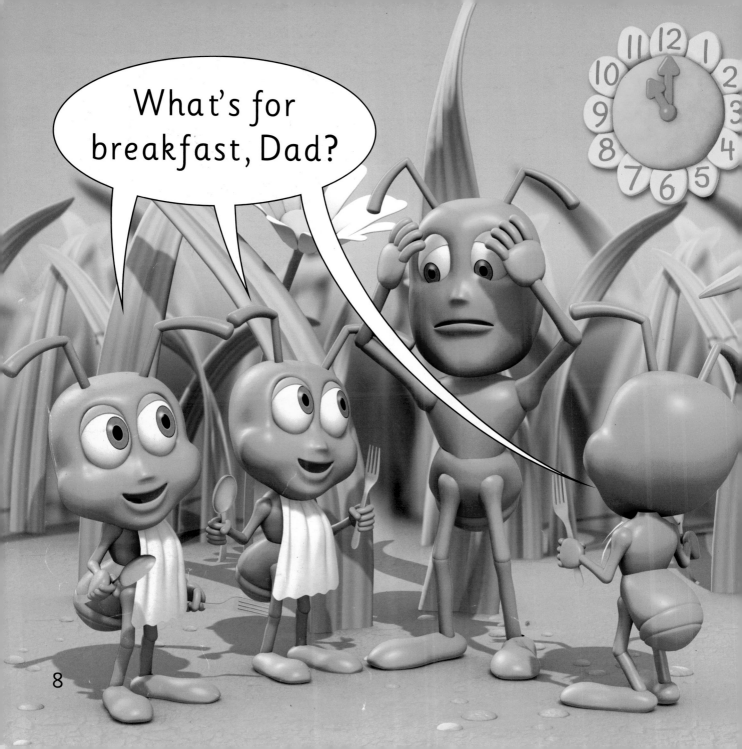

9

11

13

Dad looks for breakfast

🐾 Ideas for guided reading 🐾

Learning objectives: read high frequency words; use a variety of cues when reading; read familiar stories independently, pointing and making correspondence between written and spoken words; re-enact stories in a variety of ways; sustain attentive listening, responding to what they have heard

Curriculum links: Science – life processes and living things; Numeracy – time;

Physical Development: keeping healthy and things that contribute to this

High frequency words: for, we, like,

Interest words: breakfast, cake, yuk, chocolate, apple, yum, lunch

Word count: 36

Resources: small whiteboard and pen

Getting started

- Ask the children to name the meals of the day, and put them in order. Ask them what they enjoy eating for breakfast (some sensitivity may be required here).

- Look at the front cover and identify the creatures (ants). Ask the children what they know about ants. *What do they like to eat? (Fruit) Where do they live? (In nests in the soil).*

- Read the title using your finger to point to words as you read.

Reading and responding

- Read pp2-3 together using your finger to point to each word.

- Ask the children to look at the pictures and discuss what is happening. *Do the ants want the cake? Would this be a healthy breakfast?* Before turning the page, ask the children to predict what will happen next.

- Read pp4-5 together. Sound out the CVC word 'yuk', looking at each letter in the word, and at the picture for further clues. Encourage the children to predict what Dad will bring for breakfast next.